little Miss Dotty

by Roger Hargreaves

Welcome to Nonsenseland!

You may have heard of it!

It's where the trees are pink, orange and brown and the grass is blue!

Where dogs wear hats and birds fly backwards!

And where Little Miss Dotty lived, in the middle of Whoopee Wood.

Nonsenseland really is quite the most extraordinary place.

If you ever come across a worm wearing a straw boater and wearing a bow tie, you'll know you are in Nonsenseland!

And, if you ever happen to catch sight of a pig playing tennis, you'll know exactly where you are!

Won't you?

That's right!

Nonsenseland.

One morning, in January, Little Miss Dotty
was having breakfast.

A bowlful of marmalade, with
milk and sugar!

While she ate, she was reading the
newspaper.

She took the Nonsenseland Daily News
every day, and always read it while she ate
her dotty breakfast.

Something in the paper caught her eye!

She stopped eating and started reading.

The headline read:

'NONSENSE CUP WINNER'

And, underneath, it said:

'This year's Nonsense Cup, for the silliest idea of the year (a green tree), was yesterday awarded to Mr Silly by the King of Nonsenseland. Runners-up were Mr Muddle and Mrs Nincompoop.

'Next year', continued the story, 'the Nonsense Cup will be awarded, not for the silliest idea, but for the DOTTIEST idea of the year'.

"The dottiest idea of the year?" Little Miss Dotty thought to herself as she popped a spoonful of marmalade into her mouth. "I bet I could win that Nonsense Cup!"

After breakfast she set off for a walk in Whoopee Wood to think about this and that, but most of all to think about that famous Nonsense Cup.

On her walk she met Mr Silly.

"Congratulations on winning the Cup," she said to him.

"Oh, it was nothing really," he replied, modestly.

Little Miss Dotty thought about telling him that she was going to enter next year, but then she decided not to.

January passed.

And February.

And spring came, and the blue grass grew.

But, could Little Miss Dotty think of an idea?

She could not!

She just couldn't think of a single
dotty idea!

Summer came to Nonsenseland.

And went!

Without a single dotty idea in mind!

And the leaves started to fall from the trees.

And then, one afternoon in late November, Little Miss Dotty thought of her idea.

The dottiest idea ever!

The year ended, and January arrived in Nonsenseland.

A huge crowd gathered as usual in the Square to see who had won that year's Nonsense Cup.

The King of Nonsenseland mounted the specially built platform, and a hush descended on the crowd.

"Ladies and gentlemen," the King announced. "Again it is my pleasure to announce the annual winner of our famous Nonsense Cup."

"As you know," he continued, "the Cup will be awarded this year to whoever has had the dottiest idea of the year!"

The crowd held its breath.

"One of which," the King went on, "has been entered by Mr Nonsense!"

The crowd looked as Mr Nonsense held up his dotty idea for all to see.

A television set, with no screen!

"It's for people who don't like watching television," he explained, proudly.

The crowd clapped.

"However," continued the King, "we have an even dottier idea from last year's winner!"

Mr Silly triumphantly showed his invention to the crowd.

It was a clock!

"If you look at it in the mirror it tells you the right time," he announced.

The crowd cheered, and Mr Silly felt sure that he was going to win the Nonsense Cup for the second year running.

"But," continued the King, and Mr Silly realised that he wasn't.

"But," said the King again. "We did announce that the Nonsense Cup was to be awarded for the DOTTIEST idea of the year, and this year's winner has provided us with," he paused, "nine hundred and ninety nine DOTS!!"

Little Miss Dotty held her breath, and blushed.

"Hurrah!" roared the crowd.

"Follow me," said the King.

The King and Little Miss Dotty led the crowd through Whoopee Wood to her cottage.

And there they stopped, and stared.

Little Miss Dotty had spent the whole month of December painting dots all over her cottage. Hundreds and hundreds of different coloured dots.

Nine hundred and ninety nine to be exact.

Little Miss Dotty had counted them, very carefully.

"That's a lot of dots," remarked the King as he handed over the Nonsense Cup, and the crowd cheered.

"Thank you your Majesty," she replied, and she blused with pride.

Oh, one last thing!

If you are as good at counting dots as Little Miss Dotty, you'll be interested to know that there are one hundred and eighty three small letter 'i's in this story.

And, there are one hundred and eighty three dots on the top of all of them!

I should know!

Because I put them there!

Fantastic offers for Little Miss fans!

Collect all your Mr. Men or Little Miss books in these superb durable collectors' cases!

Only £5.99 inc. postage and packing, these wipe-clean, hard-wearing cases will give all your Mr. Men or Little Miss books a beautiful new home!

Keep track of your collection with this giant-sized double-sided Mr. Men and Little Miss Collectors' poster.

Collect 6 tokens and we will send you a brilliant giant-sized double-sided collectors' poster! Simply tape a £1 coin to cover postage and packaging in the space provided and fill out the form overleaf.

STICK £1 COIN HERE (for poster only)

Only need a few Little Miss or Mr. Men to complete your set? You can order any of the titles on the back of the books from our Mr. Men order line on 0870 787 1724. Orders should be delivered between 5 and 7 working days.

— TO BE COMPLETED BY AN ADULT —

To apply for any of these great offers, ask an adult to complete the details below and send this whole page with the appropriate payment and tokens, to: MR. MEN CLASSIC OFFER, PO BOX 715, HORSHAM RH12 5WG

☐ Please send me a giant-sized double-sided collectors' poster.
AND ☐ I enclose 6 tokens and have taped a £1 coin to the other side of this page.

☐ Please send me ☐ Mr. Men Library case(s) and/or ☐ Little Miss library case(s) at £5.99 each inc P&P

☐ I enclose a cheque/postal order payable to Egmont UK Limited for £............................

OR ☐ Please debit my MasterCard / Visa / Maestro / Delta account (delete as appropriate) for £............................

Card no. ☐☐☐☐ ☐☐☐☐ ☐☐☐☐ ☐☐☐☐ ☐☐☐☐   Security code ☐☐☐

Issue no. (if available) ☐   Start Date ☐☐/☐☐/☐☐   Expiry Date ☐☐/☐☐/☐☐

Fan's name: ....   Date of birth: ....

Address: ....

....

....   Postcode: ....

Name of parent / guardian: ....

Email for parent / guardian: ....

Signature of parent / guardian: ....

Please allow 28 days for delivery. Offer is only available while stocks last. We reserve the right to change the terms of this offer at any time and we offer a 14 day money back guarantee. This does not affect your statutory rights. Offers apply to UK only.

☐ We may occasionally wish to send you information about other Egmont children's books.
If you would rather we didn't, please tick this box.

Ref: LIM 001